S0-DOQ-772

THIS BOOK WAS DONATED

TO

𝔖𝔱. 𝔐𝔞𝔱𝔱𝔥𝔢𝔴𝔰 𝔖𝔠𝔥𝔬𝔬𝔩 𝔏𝔦𝔟𝔯𝔞𝔯𝔶

By In Honor of Vincent Oatridge

Date October 21, 1981

E
Ber

LOSING YOUR BEST FRIEND

by
CORINNE BERGSTROM

Illustrated by
PATRICIA ROSAMILIA

ST. MATTHEW'S SCHOOL
3316 Sandra Lane
Virginia Beach, Va. 23462

 **HUMAN SCIENCES PRESS**

72 Fifth Avenue   3 Henrietta Street
NEW YORK, NY 10011 ● LONDON, WC2E 8LU

*I dedicate this book to my
mother and father with love
and gratitude that they have
always been some of my best
friends.*

Copyright ©1980 by Corinne Bergstrom
Published by Human Sciences Press, 72 Fifth Avenue, New York, N.Y. 10011
All rights reserved
Printed in the United States of America
0123456789 987654321

Library of Congress Cataloging in Publication Data

Bergstrom, Corinne.
    Losing your best friend.

    SUMMARY: When she loses her best friend to a
new girl, a third grader first suffers, then learns to
adjust her life.
    [1. Friendship—Fiction] I. Rosamilia, Patricia.
II. Title.
PZ7.B45227Lo   [E]   LC   79-20622
ISBN 0-87705-471-1

Having a best friend is like having a brother or a sister. No, it's even better. Best friends are special in their own sort of way. Having a best friend and losing her can be very sad. Sometimes it's even a little scary, like going somewhere by yourself for the first time.

I know because I had a best friend. Her name was Robin. We did everything together. We rode bikes. We jumped rope. We skateboarded in summer and ice skated in winter.

We shared secrets. We even liked the same clothes. We did everything together except pretend. Robin thought it was silly to pretend, but I thought it was fun. I learned a lot when I pretended.

Sometimes I pretended that I was a guide in a national park. I told people all about the trees and animals. I learned lots of new things about nature just by studying my own backyard.

Sometimes I pretended to be a librarian. I told stories and showed pictures to little boys and girls. I helped them find books. I even checked out some of my own storybooks for them to read.

I imagined what it might be like to be in an airplane or to fly through space. I'd fly between the stars to the moon, and around and around from planet to planet.

So many times, I wished Robin would pretend with me. We
had a lot of fun doing other things, but it would have been nice if
we could have pretended together too.

Then something strange began to happen to Robin and me. Something I didn't like at all.

New neighbors moved in up the street. Sandy and Benny were twins. Sandy was in Robin's and my class at school. Benny was in the other third grade class. I asked why they weren't in the same room. Sandy said it was because schools don't want twins to be together all the time.

After school, Robin invited our new neighbors to ice skate with us. Benny couldn't come, but Sandy did. We thought we were good skaters, but Sandy made my eyes open wide. She leaped and spun like a star.

Afterwards, we went for hot chocolate. Robin and Sandy decided to start a club. Sandy would be president and Robin would be vice president. They said I could be secretary.

Robin usually stopped for me on the way to school. The next morning, she didn't come. I asked her why. She said she stopped for Sandy, instead, so they could make plans for the club.

I reminded her that I was secretary. She said it was their job to make the plans. Then I could write them down.

It didn't feel good to be left out. I felt tears coming, but I was angry, too. I didn't know if I should cry or holler.

The next day, I watched for her, but Robin didn't stop again.
She and Sandy went by. Benny was walking behind them

throwing snowballs at their backs. Maybe they couldn't stop. Or maybe they hadn't even thought about me.

At school, Miss Wilkerson asked for two volunteers to stay indoors for recess, and help her with some chores. Usually she picked Robin and me. She knew we would work hard. This time, though, she picked Robin and Sandy instead.

I asked if I might help, too. But she said she only needed two people. I know it wasn't Robin's fault, but I gave her a dirty look as I went out to the playground. I began to feel I didn't have a best friend anymore. Everything was Robin and Sandy...Robin and Sandy.

Some girls in our class were playing snow statues. I wished that I could play, too. But I was afraid to join them. Was I shy? I had never thought about it before. Robin and I had been best friends for a long time.

Then I saw Sandy's brother Benny. He was watching some boys playing tag. Would he have liked to play with them? Was he shy, too? I wanted to talk to him. But I remembered the snowballs.

Finally, recess was over. Robin said they had finished plans for the club while they were helping Miss Wilkerson. They would tell them to me after school. I felt a little better.

The first club project was a trip to the museum. Sandy's mother took us there. Robin and Sandy didn't want Benny to come, but I didn't mind. If our club had lots of people, Sandy might find another new friend. Then Robin and I could be best friends again.

At the museum, Robin and Sandy pointed at all the exhibits and laughed. There were lots of things to look at. I saw drawings of animals, and statues of Indians, pictures of cavemen all dressed in fur, and even the bones of a dinosaur.

Robin and Sandy giggled and laughed, but I didn't. I pretended I was living in the days of the dinosaurs. Terror gripped me at the thought of live monsters.

ST. MATTHEW'S SCHOOL
3316 Sandra Lane
Virginia Beach, Va. 23462

Then I dreamed I was in a tropical paradise. I was queen of the jungle. Exotic birds called me through the trees, and crocodiles moved slowly around me. Natives bowed before me and sang songs.

I glanced at Benny. His eyes had a faraway look. Was it possible that he was dreaming, too?

Robin and Sandy grabbed my arms. They wanted me to see some valuable rocks. I was glad they wanted me with them. But I missed dreaming. They would only have laughed if I had shared my thoughts.

Days passed slowly. Our club stayed the same...Robin and Sandy...except when they wanted me to do something. When they helped Miss Wilkerson at recess, no one asked me to play. One day when she asked me to help her change the bulletin board, she asked Jerry, too. All he could talk about was his new 10-speed bike. But that was better than being alone.

Then it happened.

I finally convinced Robin and Sandy that we should have others in
our club. I asked Benny to be our first new member. He was glad to join.
I was glad, too. Before long, we had eight people in our club. Maybe now
Sandy would find another friend and Robin and I would be best friends
again.

Our club decided to have a winter carnival. We divided up in groups to plan the different things the carnival would have. Here was my chance to be with Robin! But Robin wanted to work with Sandy, planning the refreshment stand.

I didn't care what I did after that. I didn't even care if I was part of the carnival at all. Then Benny suggested we do a play.

A play! I liked that. Acting was like pretending. Another girl, Pam, wanted to work with us. I wished Robin wanted to pretend just once. She might have liked it if she tried. But she didn't. And Sandy was just like her.

Our play was about a snow queen. I was really excited. I got to be the snow queen. My mother made my costume. She used an old bride's dress she found at a garage sale. It was beautiful. Pam was the snow princess. Her costume was made from ruffled curtains. We had a lot of fun practicing in them.

Benny played an evil dragon. He thought he could melt us by breathing fire. He was really fierce, and very noisy, when he played his part.

I liked Pam and Benny. We became good friends. Sandy and Robin still did everything together. But I didn't care as much as before. I had new friends, too.

Losing a best friend can be hard and hurt very much. But it's like learning to go somewhere by yourself for the first time. At times it's scary and you're not at all sure how to get there, but you go on. Soon you learn how to get there by yourself. And sometimes, you even make new friends along the way.

Our play was a big success. Now Benny, Pam, and I are planning a puppet show. We'll write the story, make and work the puppets too. And the biggest surprise of all—Sandy and Robin asked to help. That's okay with me. I can't wait to begin.